THE REPUBLIC
OF DREAMS

THE REPUBLIC OF DREAMS

A Reverie

G. GARFIELD CRIMMINS

W. W. Norton & Company • NEW YORK • LONDON

For information about permission to reproduce selections from this book, write to Permissions,
W. W. Norton & Company, Inc., 500 Fifth Avenue, New York, NY 10110.

The text of this book is composed in Geometric 231, with display set in Boca Raton.
Produced by Phoenix Offset/Hong Kong
Book design by Chris Welch Design.

Library of Congress Cataloging-in-Publication Data
Crimmins, G. Garfield.
    Republic of dreams: a reverie / G. Garfield Crimmins.
        p. cm.
    ISBN 0-393-04633-8
    I. Title.
PS3553.R514R47   1998
813'.54—dc21

98-13791
CIP

W. W. Norton & Company, Inc., 500 Fifth Avenue, New York, N.Y. 10110
http://www.wwnorton.com

W. W. Norton & Company Ltd., 10 Coptic Street, London WC1A 1PU

2 3 4 5 6 7 8 9 0

ACKNOWLEDGMENTS

⑥

My thanks to my fellow citizens: Harry Anderson, Ashley Barnes, Jerry Beisel, Heather Bryson, Peter Biela, Kate Bartoldus, Nicole Carras, Tom Chimes, Peter Frank, Freida Fehrenbacher, Bill Freeland, Jeffrey Fuller, John Hodgman, Jim Harmon, Susan Horowitz, Sandra Learner, Keith Newhouse, Judy Newhouse, Jamie O'Boyle, John Pompetti, Nancy Steel, Patrica Steigerwald, Tom Steigerwald, Edward Sargent, Pat Stewart, Lisa Smith, Bill Walton, Amy Wells, and all my other fellow citizens.

Special thanks to citizens: John W. Caldwell, John X. Crimmins, Susan Ginsburg, Claire Hankins, Chris Welch, and Alane Salierno Mason.

And for the support of The National Endowment for the Arts, the Nexus Foundation, and the Pollock-Krasner Foundation.

IMAGE ACKNOWLEDGMENTS

The author and the publisher would like to thank the following for their permission to reproduce images: Café des Artistes NYC, Becotte & Gershwin Pub., The Naturist Inc., the owners of L'indigo restaurant and the H. Henri Club, Montreal, Québec. I also have employed images from <u>L'Illustration</u>, ca. 1930; <u>National Geographic</u> magazine, 1918 through 1934; and the book <u>Die Schönheit Deines Körpers</u> (Dora Menzler, 1924). I have utilized flotsam, jetsam, and detritus found in flea markets and used book stores. I have used my own artwork as imagery. I have relied on my friends to become models to enhance the book.

Every attempt has been made to trace the sources of images. Any owners of images not credited should contact W. W. Norton & Company, Inc., 500 Fifth Avenue, New York, NY 10110, in order for a correction to be made in the next reprinting of our work.

ORPHÉE MESSENGER SERVICE

TELEGRAM

The filing time shown in the date line on telegrams and day letters is STANDARD TIME at point of origin. Time of receipt is STANDARD TIME at point of destination

LC PARIS FRANCE   1245 9 NOV 1930   OT

DR. W. PROMETHEUS

THE SMOOTH THIGHS OF ROSY COLOURED SKIES PRECEED A CRYSTAL CLEAR
NIGHT= A ONE EYED DOG WITH A CHINESE ACCENT IS ACTING AS ADVISOR=
ON THE GLASS SHELF A SILVER AEROPLANE IS EMBRACING A BILLBOARD
EDGED WITH NEON LIGHT= PROCEEDING ON SCHEDULE= GIN IS NOT COFFEE=
IN A FORTNIGHT EYES WILL SNAP SHUT LIKE AN UMBRELLA OPENING=

Y

THE COMPANY WILL APPRECIATE SUGGESTIONS FROM ITS PATRONS CONCERNING ITS SERVICE

Victor la Nuage
9 Rue de Bleu Perroquet
Polis Poeton, Q-3
la République de Rêves

POSTES REP REVES
12:00
22-VII
POLIS POETON
1984

R   6891

FPO 5

VIA AIR MAIL

RÉVERIAN LU...
R-LZ-23 PRINCE OF CLOUDS

G. Garfield Crimmins
2940 York Ave, 2-B
Philadelphia, Penn.
U.S.A.

Dear Reader,

This book is an account of my adventures and experiences on the island nation la République de Rêves, a Republic of Dreams, a nation of eccentrics, visionaries, poets, and artists. Even as I write this, I ask, do we lead two lives, one when we are awake, and another in our dreams? Before me on my desk is tangible evidence—a passport, travel tickets, maps, documents, photos, and a journal. My days and nights are filled with memories which are rich in mysteries, wonder, and the pure pleasure of living life to the fullest; these I retained when I returned to my life as G. Garfield Crimmins.

You, dear reader, you procured this book today, perhaps out of curiosity or as a diversion or because you too wish to travel in search of your other self, the one who lives in this nation of dreams. May you quickly find that other self, as I have found mine.

G. Garfield Crimmins
Philadelphia, Pennsylvania
USA

a.k.a.

Victor La Nuage
Polis Poeton
la République de Rêves

P.S. It should be understood that Rêverian French is not Franco-French. It should also be known that Rêverians are notoriously bad spellers—this being the result of the fact that Rêverians are taught to spell with images first, then with letters. The author and publisher would like to apologize in advance for any inconvenience caused by this. Good spellers are exceptions to the rule and they are treasured for their gift.

ATTENTION

VISITORS FALL UNDER THE PROTECTION OF THE
LAWS GOVERNING THE PARTICULAR, EXCEPTIONS
AND IMAGINARY SOLUTIONS, AND ARE THUS EX-
EMPT FROM THE LAWS OF TIME AND SPACE FOR
THE DURATION OF THEIR STAY. ALL VISITORS
ARE HEREBY NOTIFIED AND ADVISED THAT IT
IS UNLAWFUL TO WILLFULLY AND WITH MALICE
BRING ABOUT A DISRUPTION OR CAUSE AN UN-
WILLING TERMINATION OF THAT WHICH IS
DEEMED AND OTHERWISE RECOGNIZED AS A
VISION, DREAM OR A STATE OF POETIC INTOX-
ICATION. SUCH AN ACT IS CONSIDERED AN UN-
FORGIVABLE BREACH OF RÊVERIAN CIVILITY,
BEING CLEARLY UNCOUTH AND A SACRILEGE OF
THE HIGHEST ORDER AND IS CONSIDERED JUST
CAUSE FOR EXPULSION FROM LA RÉPUBLIQUE.

MINISTER OF IMMIGRATION
IMAGINATION AND NATURALIZATION

If a man could pass through Paradise in a dream, and have a flower presented to him as a pledge that his soul had really been there, and if he found that flower in his hand when he awoke,—Ay!—and what then?

—Samuel Taylor Coleridge

THE MIDNIGHT EXPRESS

The Midnight Express from Washington to Chicago, a luxury train smelling of leather, polished wood, and fresh flowers. A veritable land ship. Out the window of the club car, Baltimore slipped away: tangled wires and points of light, looking like the back of an old radio. Soon I was joined by a woman whose abundant honey-colored hair danced and shimmered as we talked. Her eyes were like fireflies.

She spoke excellent and precise English, but there was a trace of an accent that I could not place. Her name was Nadja La Claire. I felt sure I had known her before, felt it with a certainty more powerful than the knowledge that I was awake and not dreaming. She ordered a glass of Poet's Delight, which she said tasted of a Romantic poet's words. She offered me a sip, and I accepted. The drink sparkled, a blend of champagne and hazelnuts. When she finished her drink, she rose gracefully. "It is time, I must go; until later, G. Garfield Crimmins." She used my name as if it were an intimate joke between us. The drink and the company had me mildly intoxicated. She handed me a small yellow book. "I leave you this, <u>A Visitor's Guide to la République de Rêves</u>."

I ordered a glass of Poet's Delight, picked up the <u>Guide</u>, and while reading of Rêves, I drifted off to sleep.

I found myself on a residential tree-lined street with magnificent Victorian homes. The atmosphere was clear and crisp as I walked in the dappled sunlight, in a stillness that was otherworldly. I heard a door open and close, and a woman calling "Victor! Victor!" There was no one else on the street. She was waving and calling to me.

A VISITOR'S GUIDE TO
la République de Rêves

*B*ienvenue! Welcome! with warmth to the Rêverian Republic. Rêves is a nation overwhelmingly rich in places and things to be seen. Its cities and countrysides overflow with sites and institutions redolent of historic, intellectual, and artistic tradition. In fact there are few areas not commemorated by an artist's inspiration, a philosopher's wit, or a poet's insight.

Rêves (pronounced rev) is an island republic located in the Mid-Atlantic, somewhat south of Bermuda, between the Sea of Clouds and the Sea of the Unseen. By a majority vote of its citizens, the Republic can render itself visible or invisible, accessible or inaccessible, to the rest of the world.

The Republic guarantees freedom of thought, word, and action, as well as all of the myriad particulars of the

A ZEPPELIN ENTHUSIAST BREAKS INTO A DANCE AS AN AIRSHIP
OF THE RÊVERIAN FLEET PASSES OVERHEAD.

1

ON THE WEST COAST NEAR ABRA, NOT FAR FROM CADABRA, MAGIE.

poetic vision, to its citizens and visitors. The Rêverian culture, government, and traditions are those of bardic democracy, which is governed by poets, who draft exceptions to the rule.

The official language of Rêves is poetry, and all Rêverians are multilingual, and will understand any language you happen to speak. French, however, is the diplomatic language of choice, a nod to the rest of the world.

The population of Rêves is composed of artists, dreamers, and eccentrics who have an instinctive dislike of the narrow limitations of common sense. This is characterized by a passionate yearning toward the vague, the mystic, the invisible, and the boundless infinity of the realms of the imagination. They love love, youth, old age, beauty, splendor,

2

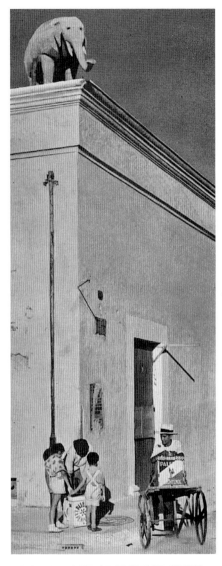

A RÊVERIAN DREAM CONTAINER AND ITS
CONTENTS.

CHILDREN SHOP AT ELEPHANT CORNER.
EFFIGIES OF ANIMALS, FRUITS AND
OBJECTS ARE SET UP AS STREET SIGNS
ON THE ROOFS OF CORNER HOUSES IN
GLASS LIONS, MALICIEUX.

POMPETTI BLVD., RENDEZVOUS.

wisdom, generosity, music, song, the feast, and the dance. They practice mischief as much as poetry, and are keenly aware that there is much in life that no ordinary logic explains; as citizen Yeats wrote, "How do we not know but that our own unreason may be better than another's truth?" A visitor once asked, "How many festivals are there in a year?" The answer was 361, an average of one festival per day (the Rêverian calendar is lunar, with thirty days in each month), though on some days festivals are augmented by feasts, ceremonies, and other celebrations.

The principal city and capital of Rêves, Polis Poeton (city of poets), is divided into quadrants surrounding Lake Eros. The River of Innocence enters Lake Eros from the west and the River of Dreams flows out eastward into the Sea of Clouds.

Each district of Polis Poeton has its own flavor, particulars, and erratic spiritual features. It is a city of contrasts, the old and the new, the familiar and the exotic. A walk through the city can take you from the charm of a Victorian neighborhood to the mystery of a North African bazaar. Paris and Berlin, not in replica but as they actually are in the imagination, are there to be found by those who seek them.

"Swarming city, city full of dreams, where the specter in broad daylight accosts the passerby," wrote Charles Baudelaire of Polis Poeton.

Accommodations vary, from the elegance of the Hotel Prince of Clouds

The Hotel Prince of Clouds on Boulevard Charles Baudelaire.

A PERFECT WAY TO END THE DAY, A DINNER AND DANCE AT MADAME
RICOCHET'S SALON AT THE INTERSECTION OF AVENUE OF QUIVERS AND
SHUDDERS AND SWEET TONGUE LANE, IN THE CAPITAL.

5

overlooking Lake Eros to the intimate Hôtel des Eccentriques on Wombat Strasse. Attractions and entertainment are plentiful. The night is alive with clubs, cafés, and theaters. Recommended are the Incomparables Club on the Boulevard Raymond Roussel, and Madame de Ricochet's Salon at the intersection of the Avenue of Quivers and Shudders and Sweet Tongue Lane. The Perpetual Public Flea Market, located on Moongate Road, is unlike any market found anywhere. One can find everything from glass nails to storytelling starfish and singing statuary. While at the market, be sure to visit the stall of Illusions and Fables, where magicians perform and relate tales from *The Book of Tormands* (the Rêverian book of sagas, myths, fables, and philosophies). Rêverians see this book, as they see all books, as a sacred source of magic, knowledge, and wisdom. Not to be missed is the Statue of Mirrors in the Botanical Gardens in the Park of the Nine Eniǵmas. (In Rêverian mythopoetry, the Nine Enigmas refer to Chance; Desire; Love; Magic; Mischief; Mystery; Time, the right and left-hand aspects; The three permanent clouds over the State of Mystère; and The heavy little box and the identity of the First Ones.)

Rêves enjoys a wide variety of temperature and atmospheric conditions that are most invigorating. In any of the various regions of the island, one can find the particulars of any of the four seasons. All meteorological manifestations occur, always locally (in miniature, as it were), within the passage of a single week. This means a hurricane can brew in your hotel's swimming pool, move out onto the street, and play itself out before advancing a block. Yet while the climatic conditions of Rêves are limitless, they can most accurately be described as temperate and as such do not always necessitate the wearing of garments. The custom of nakedness among Rêverian youth is not universally practiced but is accepted by the entire populace. When visitors encounter young citizens in a state of undress, they should delight in the aesthetic experience and remember they are in Rêves. The flora and fauna, culture, and climate vary from the mountains in Désir to the plains of Mischief and the coastal regions, with their spectacular views and inviting white sand beaches.

Inter-Rêves travel is easy, and it can begin at any hour of the day or night by railway, dirigible, aeroplane, or a convertible motorcar. One can begin on a summer day in the capital and spend a winter evening in the provinces in a matter of hours, without concern for cost or time.

Motor through the Rêverian plains and wooded hills on a splendid network
of paved roadways radiating in various directions from Polis Poeton.

In Small Shadows residential quarter, the natives come out to
look and eat air.

The Oneiro (Greek for "dream") is the denomination for coinage and currency in Rêves. The possession of this currency provides one with the means to exchange goods, services, and dreams.

Literacy and cultural participation are universal on the island of Rêves.

Books, works of art, and musical recordings are the gifts of choice for any occasion. The nation's wealth and resources are evenly distributed. Its society is remarkably egalitarian and free of any sort of crime. However, Rêves is not a utopia, but a topospoetic.

9

Cloud Oak Commemorative

Located throughout Rêves are tracts of cloud oaks. These trees manufacture
lighter-than-air gases which keep their branches buoyant. As they approach
maturity their trunks and root systems atrophy and become epiphytic in
nature, dependent on the atmosphere for nourishment. Occasionally in
extreme old age a tree will sever its contact with the ground entirely and
drift off to found a new colony. These trees are revered for their beauty
and also as a constant source of fuel for Rêverian dirigibles.

Ministry of Postes and Telegraphs

Postal stamps serve a dual function for Rêverians. The stamps alone or in
combination can carry a message, ask a question, or make a request. They
also function in a normal capacity to pay for the cost of postage.
The above examples may be interpreted as it is time to send a letter, by
air, or then again could be saying something else altogether. Like many
things Reverian, appearances can be deceiving.

While the Republic is a modern nation, its multiethnic traditions are woven into the fabric of its society. The islanders practice a trancelike state of awake dreaming called "Droomall." In this state they describe themselves as moving into a realm in which the mind and the spirit flow outward into the natural immensity of things. The practitioner's privilege of solitude is sacrosanct and is protected by law and custom.

Rêverians are descended from a race older than that which now dominates the globe, and are born and found in all the many lands of the world. In appearance, there is scarcely a perceptible difference from the general

A CITIZEN OF THE VILLAGE RISK, IN THE PROVINCE OF AMOUR, PRACTICING "DROOMALL" (A TRANCELIKE STATE OF AWAKE DREAMING).

populace in which they are born, but they are marked by having an exceptionally fertile imagination verging on hallucinations. Their sense of humor is eccentric and at times sardonic. In these ways they identify their true nature and origin. On the island of Rêves, they consider themselves a tribe of artists, dreamers, eccentrics, poets, and tellers of tales. Foreign-born Rêverians have the right of gaining citizenship by establishing their essential character on Rêves, or by providing appropriate documentation to a Rêverian embassy or consulate.

"We are all inventors, we are all dreamers, mutually creating and dreaming each other and telling each other our dreams." And then he asked, "Are we the one that is dreaming or are we a part of someone else's dream?"
— The Book of Tormands,
Vol. III, Chapter 2

RÊVERIANS CONSIDER
THEMSELVES A TRIBE OF
ARTISTS, DREAMERS,
ECCENTRICS, POETS, AND
TELLERS OF TALES.

13

Of the 53.9 million Rêverians dispersed throughout the world, perhaps fewer than many live permanently on Rêves. While Rêverians consider themselves a single race by imagination and tradition, they take pride in their variations of color, height, and foot size. Rêverians are especially fond of the following quote from *The Book of Tormands:* "The new moon and the full moon are both completely the moon. But who could love the moon as much if it did not change?"

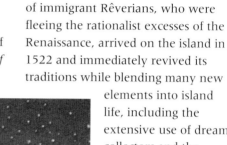

Rêves claims to be the oldest continuous republic, but because it remained isolated (hidden) until 1928, this claim is often ignored in conventional histories. The Rêverian Republic began at about 700 B.C. O.T. (ordinary time) along the shores of the Adriatic when the poet Anrig the Great discovered that the truth of dreams could form the basis of a new society.

The history of the island between 9 A.D. and 1522 O.T. remains a mystery. According to archaeological records, the island was vacated sometime between 1360 and the arrival of the second Rêverian settlers. The most convincing theory suggests the Rêverians lost track of time, since they calculated things by the shape of clouds, by shadows, by the flight of birds, by throwing bones over their left shoulders, and by every kind of trick and game of chance that you could put a mind to. The second wave of immigrant Rêverians, who were fleeing the rationalist excesses of the Renaissance, arrived on the island in 1522 and immediately revived its traditions while blending many new elements into island life, including the extensive use of dream collectors and the practice of Droomall.

Recently discovered documents in which the original Rêverians referred to themselves as "Randomites" suggests a connection with the Randomites, a society of nonlinear thinkers active in the 1920s. Their membership was international, as was their persecution and suppression by linear thinkers of the period. By 1938, nothing more was heard of them and all traces of their activities had vanished.

Because the island lies in proximity to trade and travel routes, occasional military expeditions attempted to conquer the Republic. None of these forces was ever successful, and none ever returned to its home country. It now appears that these armies were

Himself, Anrig the Great, poet, philosopher, reluctant leader,
storyteller, and liar.

A CAMOUFLAGED AEROPLANE OF THE CORPS AËRONAUTIQUE.

absorbed into the general population; coming to conquer, they were conquered. The Sûreté Nationale, the Rêverian police, is a small force, about twenty; the exact number is unknown. Qualifications include a repulsion to belonging to any military or quasi-military organization. Its chief function is to prevent the unlawful interference with dreams.

In the 1880s, the Republic began to experience a period of internal strife caused by a band of citizens who, under the banner of common sense, sought to impose their collective dream on the entire nation. The "Unpleasantness," which lasted until 1889, when poetic order was restored, is referred to simply as "The Bad Dream." Established after the Unpleasantness, the Républicain Garde exist as guardians of the dream; provide a reason to dress up, have parades, and express patriotic feelings; perform ceremonial duties for official occasions; and perform sundry other domestic activities.

Between 1900 and 1923, countless

RÊVERIAN GENERALS AND ADMIRALS READY TO PARADE.

numbers of Rêverians established themselves as operatives for the Republic internationally, committed to keeping the flame of the imagination alive and sabotaging the preponderance of linear thinking. They continue to meet with only limited success.

17

I awoke to the voices and banter of my fellow travelers. I no longer heard the clatter of wheels on tracks. Now, the movement was a gentle vibration of churning engines. I looked out the window; one eye saw a landscape, the other a seascape.

"There is nothing that can compare with travel on the night ferry, riding in the luxury of <u>la première classe</u>. The seascape in the light of the full moon is extraordinary, yes?" commented a small, well-dressed man sitting next to me, who, oddly enough, reminded me of myself when I was younger. Then I saw, in a reflection of the window, an island materialize on the horizon.

In the morning I stepped out onto the ship's deck, glittering under the golden sun. As the ship entered a lake, I was greeted by the vast panorama of a city with red-tiled roofs dotted among the green of trees. The lake waters danced in the sunlight, and on the quay people waved merrily. Overhead a dirigible drifted. I took a deep breath, inhaling the smell of flowers and clean air and music. After disembarking, I began to stroll. The shadows were long, the air was crisp, and the sun's rays were like warm fingers of desire. A cat passed me; its face was familiar, and it advised me in a voice like fine tobacco to continue on, for I was expected and would be received.

The architecture was a strange mix, an eccentric blend of cultures. On Upper West Wind, with its tidy gardens and extremely polite people who spoke in puns, I felt as if I were in England. As I turned onto the rue la Rime et la Raison, I might have been in Paris. In sidewalk cafés, cosmopolitan men and women sipped espresso and spoke in verse. Down one wide avenue, there was a procession of bagpipes, with baby carriages following at a respectful distance.

I took a seat at a café that overlooked a small park, where an orchestra was playing. At another table there was an attractive young woman reading a book. Her breasts were bare, and her long golden hair was neatly braided only on one side, while the other side hung loose and wild. When she noticed me she closed

her book and smiled. As she rose, I saw that she wore a shimmering purple sarong around her waist. In a sensuous fluid stride she came over to my table.

"Good morning, monsieur. Would you care for some coffee?"

"Yes, and a croissant, please."

From the park across the street the strains of Beethoven's "Ode to Joy" drifted into the café. A crowd began to gather around the musicians, who wore bowler hats emblazoned with a white question mark on the crown. The waitress arrived with my order and said, "On the house, monsieur, in honor of the Feast of the Hungry Eye." The coffee had the flavor of freshly roasted beans, which I savored like a fine wine. The croissant was so buttery and flaky it melted in my mouth. This satisfied my hunger.

I was continuing my stroll down the Avenue of Soft Winds when suddenly clouds gathered overhead, the air grew still, and the sun dissolved as thunder roared and rumbled through the purple sky, followed by blazing fingers of light. A great blanket of water descended, followed by a soft warm rain. Applauding and smiling people ran out into the street and began to dance in the rainy bath, lovers embraced, and children splashed in pools of water on the street.

On the rue du Bleu Perroquet, I stopped to get a paper, the English-French edition of <u>Le Communiqué</u>, the daily newspaper. The first item was "Poem of the Day," followed by an instructive editorial which began, "If M. or Mme. Numero Neuf suddenly appear at a street corner and recognize you, stop and do not laugh. They will give you a heavy little box."

Then on the second page in bold type, an article about a tourist found dead in the Park of Limpid Solitude, wearing two sets of clothing down to his under-wear—the first recorded homicide in the Republic in two hundred years, since the infamous X case in 1736. I stopped reading and looked at the date at the top of the paper: 14 mai 1936. Unless I was dreaming, this "news" was a half-century old. My eyes fell back to the article:

"The murdered man was found to be carrying two sets of identification: one for a G. Garfield Crimmins. . . ." I felt an involuntary shudder; then reached into "through the eyes of poets"

Le Communiqué

Polis Poeton, la République de Rêves

14 mai 1936

POEM OF THE DAY

Noonday

The pencil made
marks
    The marks became
words
    The words became
flesh
    The flesh became
fingers
    The fingers became
eyes
    The eyes became
ears
    The ears became the
mouth
    and the nose laughed and
said, "This is not to be
understood, this shivering and
squiggling of words on clouds
like paper."

La Gioconda en Rêves

The Pleasures of the Glove

Fruit of the Dream

The night offers a special atmosphere like the pleasure
of seeing a spoon and the wheel of a bicycle receive the
gift of speech.

Andre stands by the window watching the clouds pass-
ing rapidly by like the hands of a clock gone mad. The
door opens to present an evening walk he accepts. He
strolls alone as always. He enters the zone of the unknown beyond instantly the mysterious region where the
past and future are performed in the heart of the present. By the River of Innocence he stops, a tree laughs
like a spider, he studies the reflections of the night. A
strange luminosity is emanating from beneath the surface
of the water.

Without delay Andre enters the river. A starfish passes
holding hands with a petrified bird. There is a soft silence and it has a delightful smell. From behind a rock
of freshly cut wood can be heard the amorous exchange
of a sewing machine and its lover the umbrella. A woman like a poem of wet clay moves toward him. Her hair
is dark like the leaves of a tall blonde tree. Her eyes are
blue like black coffee. She speaks with words of
intoxication and intelligence. A pleasant electro-
magnetic storm begins to sing in his head. He is enticed
to move closer to better taste the words. He studies her
closely her eyes are closed and her breast exposed. Her
face resembles an exiled angel and she is beautiful like a
road map of the heavens. His senses are disordered and
he is astounded and she melts before he can speak.

Moving on slightly askew, he remembers a time past
when on the islands of Hallucinations in an invisible
hour he had learned to domesticate the sewing machine.
The table had laughed and he wondered if it still

continued on page 6

Qui suis-je? Si par exception je m'en
rapportais à un adage : en effet pourquoi
tout ne reviendrait-il pas à savoir qui je
« hante »? Je dois avouer que ce dernier
mot m'égare, tendant à établir entre cer-
tains êtres et moi des rapports plus sin-
guliers, moins évitables, plus troublants
que je ne pensais. Il dit beaucoup plus

FRENCH ENGLISH
EDITION

TWO RÊVERIAN MAIDENS ENJOY A ROUND OF PONG.

La République de Rêves

LICENCE POÉTIQUE

CARTE D'IDENTITÉ

nom

adresse

ville

province

nationalité

John Pomppett

Ministère de la Poésie

N° 2331

my coat and took out my passport. The gold crest of la République de Rêves was embossed on its tan cover. Opening it, I found my picture and the name Victor La Nuage, born 9 fevrier 1915 in Tower of Winds, Hasard, la République de Rêves.

The sounds of the city had become muffled and distant; I was enveloped in utter stillness and quiet. Then, like a snap of fingers, the sounds returned. I was still standing on the corner with the paper clutched in my hands.

I folded the newspaper and put it under my arm and calmly made my way to 9 rue du Bleu Perroquet. The building was set back from the street, a mission-style gleaming white stucco with a red-tiled roof. I tried the door and found it open, and by instinct went to the second floor.

Opening the door to 2-B, I entered a spacious but cluttered room. The north wall was lined with a bulging floor-to-ceiling walnut bookcase, and there were papers and books on all the tables. Fanciful sculptures adorned the fireplace mantel. The east and west walls held paintings of nudes in surreal settings and enigmatic

narratives. A large bay window was set in the south wall with a splendid view of Lake Eros. Beside the French doors that led to the balcony were two large plants with vibrant, flame-colored trumpet blooms. On the desk set in the bay, I found a neat stack of letters. One with a return address for the *Société de Prometheus* on rue de Sweet Escape looked official. I sat down and found a letter opener.

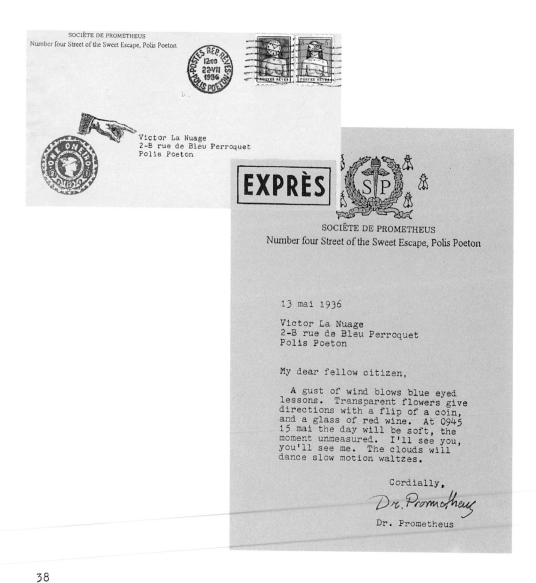

SOCIÉTE DE PROMETHEUS
Number four Street of the Sweet Escape, Polis Poeton

Victor La Nuage
2-B rue de Bleu Perroquet
Polis Poeton

EXPRÈS

SOCIÉTE DE PROMETHEUS
Number four Street of the Sweet Escape, Polis Poeton

13 mai 1936

Victor La Nuage
2-B rue de Bleu Perroquet
Polis Poeton

My dear fellow citizen,

A gust of wind blows blue eyed lessons. Transparent flowers give directions with a flip of a coin, and a glass of red wine. At 0945 15 mai the day will be soft, the moment unmeasured. I'll see you, you'll see me. The clouds will dance slow motion waltzes.

Cordially,

Dr. Prometheus

Dr. Prometheus

Suddenly the door opened again and beside me was the woman who had called to me in my dream. I knew her name without thinking—Nadja. She took my hand, squeezed it softly, and whispered, "Let's get a drink."

We walked up to the old city along rue de Quivering Shadows, then found a café on Hand in Hand Avenue and sat down and ordered some wine. There were musicians playing across the street and people dancing all around us. They would celebrate until morning and then start all over again to celebrate the Feast of the Walking Statues.

The wine had a mellow fruity flavor of Chianti, a liquid poem. Nadja leaned over the table and whispered, "Remember and somewhere in your memory, you know. The old Rêverians discovered that time does not flow in just one direction. It moves right, left, backwards, and forwards. They learned how to use this knowledge to begin time travel. Ordinary time exists for most of the world. Here

in Rêves, we see time differently." We finished and went to a nearby park on the shore of Lake Eros. On the Promenade des Amants, a boardwalk that overlooked Lake Eros, there was a comfortable light breeze coming off the water.

Soon we came upon a golden oak tree. Its boughs came down to the ground, completely hiding its trunk. Nadja took my hand and led me under it. "Remember this tree, Victor?" Her wrap dropped and her bare breasts gleamed in the half-light. We embraced, kissed, and entered the realm of unmeasured time.

Later, back in the flat, I saw a framed photo of Nadja and myself on the desk that I had not noticed before. Memories overtook me and I fell into a state of Droomall: the Rêverian proverb "Cast your heart out, then run and catch it" suffused my mind. The flat was dark when I returned from Droomall. The night birds were singing. I slipped into bed next to Nadja, snuggling close to her comforting nakedness, and sleep overtook me like a warm bath. Just as I dropped into sleep, I remembered: I had a 0945 appointment with Dr. Prometheus.

DR. PROMETHEUS

"**N**umber four Street of Sweet Escape," I told the taxi driver. "I once picked up Raymond Roussel on that exact corner," he said as he pulled away from the curb, "and he had the same destination as you."

He continued talking, not waiting for an answer. He was happy to talk, and I to listen.

"Monsieur Roussel wrote of his stay in Trembling Star, a village in Temps on the northwest coast—it's in one of the guidebooks." Without missing a beat he launched into the story.

"He discovered that the inhabitants corresponded by means of sponges.

When they wish to speak from a distance, they speak closely to one of these sponges, then they send them to their friends. When the friends receive the sponges, they press them softly and their friends' most intimate words come out of them like water." As he finished we were rounding Faustroll Circle. In its center stood a magnificent building of grand proportions. "That's the Palace of Imagination," the driver offered, "where in 1911 Apollinaire's <u>The Breasts of Tiresias</u> had its debut in open air—there were red and blue balloons in the sky for weeks." We then turned onto a tree-lined Boulevard of Splendid Food and Fine Wine. At the intersection of the Slumbering Poet and Sweet Escape, I paid my fare, got out of the cab, and wished the driver "Au revoir."

THE PALACE OF IMAGINATION, FAUSTROLL CIRCLE.

"In dreams and by chance," he replied.

Number 4 had a massive bronze door. Inscribed across the portal was the cryptic poem "BRILLIANT MIRRORS WRITHE LIKE FLAGS, THE SHADOWS QUIVER LIKE QUICKSILVER, THE CLOCKS ARE ON HOLIDAY." At the reception desk I asked how I might find the Société de Prometheus. I walked down a large gallery engulfed in medieval dusk. Pygmy aircraft hung from the ceiling, sculptures whose eyes seemed to follow me as I passed by. In the center was a life-size replica of the Bride of the Wind, the ship that rediscovered the island of Rêves in 1522: a placard said it had been constructed "using mirrors, bones of honey bees, scissors, spun glass, and a telegraph pole." A display case nearby held the ship's log, open to 20 August 1521: "We are in the Sea of Bicycle Wheels, alive with fish of all colors. The air is magnetic and the hair of the waves is long and trembles like luminous emblems of desire." And on the facing page: "1 September. 103 degrees Fahrenheit, the sea boils. We have drifted three days and three nights. We hide in the shadows and make ice. But this catches fire. We wait for evening." Finally I came to a door with a small brass plate marked "private," and below it the insignia of the Société with the inscription:

THE SOCIETY IS AN ORGANIZATION VISIBLE, INVISIBLE, SECRET, AND SUBVERSIVE, WHOSE
CHARGE IS TO REVEAL THE MYSTERY OF THE VISIBLE NEVERSEEN, TO BRING
TO THE SURFACE THE TRUTH OF THE INNER EYE, UNREASON AND REASON, TO BRING
ABOUT AND PERPETUATE THE MARVELOUS. WE BELIEVE THE DESIRE FOR WONDERS
TO BE THE ESSENCE OF THE HUMAN SPIRIT.

I pushed the buzzer, and the door opened. We entered a room of subdued light coming through Venetian blinds. Two French doors opened onto a garden courtyard in full bloom around a pond with gurgling water. On one wall were bookcases and a desk. Over the desk was a large painting depicting a battle scene, in which a large mass of uniformed soldiers, under a flag of black and white with an emblem of a clock, were being defeated by a bizarre band of men and women, young and old, in colorful costumes, some dressed and others totally

naked. Their weapons, instead of the spears and arrows of their opponents, were musical instruments, leaping dogs and cats, and flying fish. They fought under a tricolored flag of red, yellow, and blue with a white spiral in the center. On another wall were maps and on another, framed sepia photographs; the color of memories.

"Bonjour, Victor," Dr. Prometheus said, extending his hand, and greeted me warmly. We sat at a table by the window. He took out a cigarette case and offered me one, which I accepted. His buff metal lighter had a raised

emblem consisting of a ball, a bird, and an anchor and the words SEMPER FIDELIS.

"No doubt, G. Garfield Crimmins, you have realized by now that you are Victor La Nuage, a Rêverian citizen. On a mission for the Société, in ordinary time, you assumed the identity of G. Garfield Crimmins, believed to be a member of the League of Common Sense, in order to infiltrate the League."

"I was on my way to Chicago. I am supposed to be there today," I said meekly.

"Your other appointment has been canceled," Dr. Prometheus said with assurance.

THE KEEPER OF MIRRORS LEADS THE CONCLUSIVE CHARGE OF THE RÊVERIAN IRREGULARS AGAINST
THE INTERNATIONAL BRIGADE OF THE DEFENDERS OF COMMON SENSE.
—FROM THE BOOK OF TORMANDS, RÊVERIAN SAGAS, VOL. VI, LEAF #16

He got up, went to a cabinet, and poured some brandy into two glasses. I
sipped my brandy as he continued. "We believe that two agents from the League
of Common Sense are on the island. They may be after you, but there is no need
for concern. You will be protected and will receive instructions. And remember,"
he raised his glass, "the fabric of the adorable unlikelihoods must become finer as
one advances." He reached into his vest pocket and presented me with a small,
light-red cloth-bound book and put it on the table. On the cover, in tarnished
gold, were the words "National Journal 1932." I turned it over in my hands and

felt its familiarity. "You left it on the night ferry," he said.

Back outside, the green grass and trees were effervescent and glistening as shafts of light broke through. I started down toward the Boulevard of Splendid Food and Fine Wine, off Sweet Escape, and saw across the roadway the enchanted beauty of Park of Limpid Solitude. To get there I crossed the street, where steam was rising from the asphalt, stepping over little pools of water. Everything was quiet and still. I could hear the leaves dance in the breeze, feel the water of Lake Eros licking the shore. Alone with myself, I took a gold oneiro coin from my pocket. One dream, I thought as I skipped it out across the still surface, which held a mirror image of the face of the noonday sun.

I continued on to the Park of Smiles and Runaway Eyes. Among the strollers, a naked young couple moved lazily along. On Mad Swan Lane there was an impromptu dance. Crowds of people lined the street for a parade of tricolored flags, banners, a bagpipe band, and nude young men carrying a statue of the Muse Whisper.

STROLLERS IN THE PARK OF
SMILES & RUNAWAY EYES.

IMPROMPTU DANCE, MAD SWAN LANE, THE CAPITAL.

THE MUSE WHISPER, GUARDIAN AND PATRON OF THE SOCIÉTÉ.

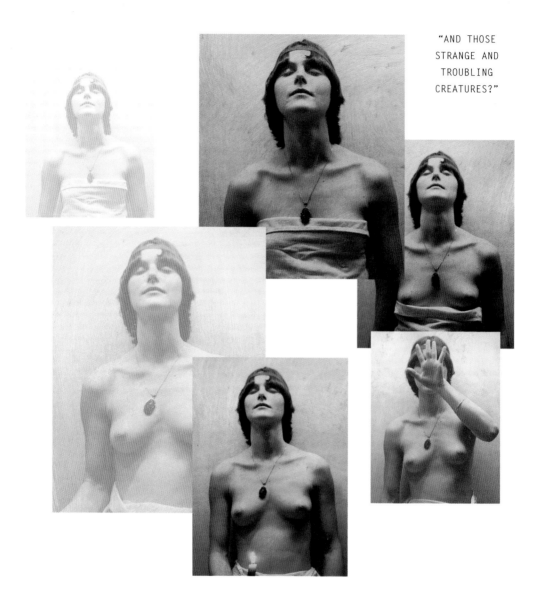

Back at my flat, I sat quietly at my desk smoking a cigarette, watching the smoke rise and dissolve in the fading light. I turned on the lamp and opened the journal.

13 janvier 1932

I met with Dr. P. The League of Common Sense have stepped up attacks on our allies, the Randomites: the society of nonlinear thinkers. I will be joining them in an operation to sabotage the LOCS activities in Philadelphia. Nadja will be part of the team.

⑥

14 janvier 1932

Polis Poeton. We arrived before dawn, the zeppelin hovering above the ground, the motors of the <u>Daedalus</u> slowly turning. As we boarded an airshipman escorted us to our cabin. We lifted off. Gliding north over the Magnetic Fields, we could see Polis Poeton behind us in the distance, glistening like a jewel surrounding the waters of Lake Eros. We passed over Glass Lions, Tall Towers, then over the snow-capped peaks of Mount Adonis. To our left, Mount Venus glowed rosy in the morning sun. Below us, the South Atlantic was a vast glittering desert. As an airshipman inspected our passports, his language drifted from Italian, to English, to French, to German. I will miss the sound of the many languages of Rêves.

⑥

20 January 1935 O.T.

We arrived at Lakehurst at dawn. The crowds that greeted us were jubilant. There were joyful shouts at the wonder of the <u>Daedalus,</u> and its vast size, which was larger than a luxury liner of the high seas. The weather was as brisk as that of the Rêverian Alps: cold but comfortable.

Was this a trick? Was I the subject of some kind of experiment? I felt as if I were in a cinema, watching a film in which I was one of the characters. The words evoked vivid, clear memories. Remembering the Doctor's words, "Memory and imagination are two sides of the same coin," I took a sip of brandy and picked up the journal again. The entry was dated 26 January O.T. On the edge of a dream, I turned the page.

26 January 1935 O.T.
Philadelphia, I met O'Boyle today, an imposing fellow: Tall with a black patch over one eye, flaming red hair and a beard. He greeted me by saying, "Welcome to the land of greed and common sense." I liked him immediately. He is a native born Rêverian, I can see it in his eye. I remembered that he had been one of the signers of the Rêverian Proclamation. He offered me brandy, and we sat and chatted about the plight of the Randomites. He gave me a wrist-watch and apologized, explaining that here, keeping time is as important as eating.

(6)

27 January 1935 O.T.
Today at O'Boyle's apt., I met with the team: Austin Vee, Nadja, and Margo. The operation's code name is Trojan Clock. We along with nine Randomites will attend a ceremony at the League's head-quarters in the guise of LOCS members. We are to disrupt the meeting. We will have cap guns that look and feel like real pistols and champagne-filled water pistols.

(6)

28 January 1935 O.T.
In the great Hall of Common Sense, pompous speeches by officials. The LOCS president presented miniature bronze duplicates of two oversized grandfather clocks. He began a speech about the respon-sibility of the LOCS to protect the ideals and philosophies of Com-mon Sense, in its battle against the loathsome Randomites. "We

should see the clock as symbol of our ideals, as a guide for conducting our lives, and a constant reminder of the unadulterated logic of time. . . ." His speech was interrupted by the chimes of the grandfather clocks. At exactly 9:13, two naked youths, one male, one female, emerged from the clocks, wearing clock-face masks. The audience sat in stunned silence as the two began an erotic dance. Then the Randomites stood up as one and scattered around the hall, squirting people with champagne and firing their cap guns into the air, shouting: "Long live the Imagination! Liberty! Love! Poetry!" There followed a hushed silence; and then it began. A riot, complete and utter chaos, broke out in the hall. A surging sea churned by a storm of anger. At the height of it my hand was hit by a hurled

object, and my cap gun, which I had dropped and only just retrieved, inadvertently fired. I watched in horror as I saw a man fall. I saw the blood, the look of disbelief and pain on his face. I saw him fall to the floor. I knew that he was dead.

I stopped reading. I remembered it all. My gun must have been switched with a pistol containing live ammunition. Flooded with sorrow, I looked out the open window and saw the lights of the city glittering like jewels in the night. Their reflection rippled in the waters of Lake Eros like an echo. I could hear laughter and music from the cafés and clubs floating in on a soft breeze. I forced myself to read on.

1 February 1935 O.T.
Philadelphia
J have taken refuge in the Rêverian consulate. The Randomites were of course blamed in the death of Gerald G. Crimmins. Though he was in fact a Randomite, the League claimed him as one of their own, and made him a martyr. Nadja has been recalled to the island. J am not able to accompany her because both the League and the police are looking for me, and my description has been published in the papers.

(6)

5 February 1935 O.T.
Philadelphia
Saturday, clear, and windy; a few stray clouds race across the blue sky. J have been closeted in a secluded second-floor room at the Rêverian consulate. The flag snaps and billows in the stiff breeze. The papers have begun to lose interest in the story of my where-abouts. They are filled instead with more current articles, all depressing.

(6)

ORPHÉE MESSENGER SERVICE
TELEGRAM

CLASS OF SERVICE

This is a full-rate Telegram or Cablegram unless its deferred character is indicated by a suitable symbol above or preceding the address.

SYMBOLS

DL=Day Letter
NL=Night Letter
LC=Deferred Cable
NLT=Cable Night Letter
Ship Radiogram

The filing time shown in the date line on telegrams and day letters is STANDARD TIME at point of origin.   Time of receipt is STANDARD TIME at point of destination

```
LC POLIS POETON                    1345 12 FEB. 1935 OT
VICTOR LA NUAGE

THE EYE OF THE TELEPHONE IS SILENT: THE OWL OF MINERVA TAKES
FLIGHT: THE SHADES OF NIGHT HAVE FALLEN: DECAPITATE THE BLUE
COMET AT ONCE: R-LZ-37 DAEDALUS AWAITS: TARDINESS IS NOT TOL-
ERATED: PROCEED AS THE CROWS FLY: INSTRUCTIONS IN THE CONTAIN-
ER LABELED "MORNING" AS INDICATED: THE DAY IS ORANGE THE HOUR
IS GREEN:

                              DR. PROMETHEUS
```

THE COMPANY WILL APPRECIATE SUGGESTIONS FROM ITS PATRONS CONCERNING ITS SERVICE

12 February 1935 O.T.

Philadelphia

I received a telegram from Dr. P. today. I'm to leave on the airship _Daedalus_, for home, Nadja, and the unguarded faces of my fellow Rêverians. After two weeks in this room, the days have melted into each other. Although I have been well cared for I still have felt like a prisoner, but the telegram has lifted my spirits immeasurably.

⑥

I drifted into a memory: Nadja and I strolling hand in hand on the Promenade des Amants, winding through a park where couples danced cheek to cheek.

Then a meeting with Dr. Prometheus, stylish in his white linen suit, a bright red carnation in his lapel, saying, "Victor, the Society and the Central Bureau have decided on another mission. If you decide that you want to participate, you will have to go through training that will take you forward in ordinary time to 1978. You will assume the identity of G. Garfield Crimmins, the son of the man that you have accidentally killed." He paused. "You will bring Crimmins back to the island with you, setting in motion a series of irrational events which will scramble the future plans of the LOCS. And in doing this, you will also save Crimmins, who has been targeted by the League for termination, and thus atone for the death of his father."

⑥

A loud chirping from a mockingbird brought me into consciousness. It was just before dawn: the first rays of sunlight appeared on the rooftops of the city. The journal lay on the floor beside my desk. Half awake, half asleep, I wondered, had

I been dreaming or had I been reading? I picked up the journal, and leafing through it I found a LOCS broadsheet folded and tucked between two pages. I stared into nothingness, a question between two mirrors facing each other.

I went in search of a café. In a small garden park, a young couple, bare to the waist, wore colorful sarongs. He was on one knee, serenading the young lady with throat singing. She had a flower behind her right ear. She was looking and she was smiling. It felt like something was going to happen, it was a full moon. The singing stopped and the couple embraced. Another couple passed by on a prancing zebra on a mission of erotic navigation. By the statue of the Muse of Shadows, an elderly gentleman sang about love. I took a seat at a café, ordered coffee, and glanced at the <u>Le Communiqué</u> that I had picked up. On the front page was another piece about the homicide in the park. Had I, Victor, somehow been responsible for the death of another Crimmins, the same one I was supposed to save? And why then hadn't Dr. Prometheus told me he was dead? When my coffee arrived I put aside my paper. On the table next to my cup was a letter, and beneath that, a telegram.

ORPHÉE MESSENGER SERVICE

TELEGRAM

CLASS OF SERVICE	SYMBOLS
This is a full-rate Telegram or Cablegram unless its deferred character is indicated by a suitable symbol above or preceding the address.	DL = Day Letter
	NL = Night Letter
	LC = Deferred Cable
	NLT = Cable Night Letter
	Ship Radiogram

The filing time shown in the date line on telegrams and day letters is STANDARD TIME at point of origin. Time of receipt is STANDARD TIME at point of destination

LC POLIS POETON   1645 20 MAI 1936
VICTOR LA NUAGE

SHIPMENT RECEIVED: LIGHT A CANDLE THE SCULPTURES HAVE LEFT
THEIR PEDESTALS: 2200 HOURS: RROSE SELEVAY: YOUR REFLECTION
AWAITS: REMEMBER YOUR HAT: GIN IS NOT COFFEE THE WINE IS RED:
EYES WILL SHUT LIKE AN UMBRELLA OPENING: TURN THE CLOCK BACK:

                              DR. PROMETHEUS

Dear Victor,
I have rooms at the House of the Mathematician, on the Street of
Lost Thoughts. I have only been here for a short time, and I am
overwhelmed and astonished by everything. I thought I saw you on
the night ferry, but you did not seem to recognize me. I found your
journal left behind on your seat and returned it to Dr. Prometheus.
I hope it is now in your possession. Until tomorrow, with the
Doctor. . . ."
Cordially,
G. Garfield Crimmins.

When I arrived at the Doctor's office, G. Garfield was already there. He looked at me with a steady gaze. "I once dreamed the dreams in your journal entries," he said.

The Doctor entered and motioned for us to sit down. His eyes moved from me to G. Garfield; he sat and placed his hands in front of his chest with his fingertips touching. He spoke slowly and deliberately. "You are familiar with the term 'doppelgänger,' yes? But neither of you is a doppelgänger. You are the same person: you, Victor, in Rêverian time, G. Garfield in ordinary time."

"Then I killed my father!" G. Garfield said in a trembling voice.

"Not exactly," Dr. Prometheus responded calmly. "You and Victor are the same person and at the same time two different people. You exist on separate planes. G. Garfield, you dream of Victor, and Victor dreams of you. If either of you were to cease to exist, then so would the other. But though your dreams are the same, your actions, when awake, are distinct."

The Doctor rose and went to a cabinet, returning with a bottle and three snifters. The silence was profound, the garden was still, and the room was filled by the haze of smoke, pierced by a shaft of sunlight. "G. Garfield, the League of Common Sense wants you either dead or reassimilated back into a "rational, normal individual.' They have pursued you here; they have even reported your murder to the papers. Foolishly, they believe that life imitates not art, but the directives of common sense." Outside, a soft breeze rose and fell; the leaves rustled. Dr. Prometheus smiled. "We, however, know the opposite to be the case. Gentlemen, your mission is to go your own ways and indulge your fantasies for the next several days. Trust that you will be safe. You will hear from me often."

PROCLAMATION OF THE RÊVERIAN RÉPUBLIQUE

Rêverians! The World! In the name of Liberty, Love and Poetry, and in the luminous shadows of generations past from which we receive the traditions and visions of Rêves, the Rêverian nation through this document summons its citizens to the flag and declares its existence to the larger world.

We declare our presence, our philosophies, our art and our eccentric nature to the unfettered control of the Rêverian destinies to be sovereign and indefeasible and that all generations, past, present and future have asserted these rights and our continuum as a state. We hereby proclaim and acknowledge La République de Rêves as a sovereign, independent nation and pledge a portion of our dreams to its existence, its freedom, its welfare and to its exaltation among the nations.

The République guarantees freedom, liberty of thought, word and action and the myriad of particulars of the poetic to all its citizens, and makes known its resolve to uphold and pursue the prosperities of all, cherishing the extraordinary, the marvellous, eliminating inertness, boredom and the conventions of common sense, reason and logic. We pledge to bring forth the more noble and effervescent, dazzling sense of poetic reason and logic.

We place the spirit and the survival of the République under the protection of the oneiromancy of its citizens which we cause to permeate and let guide our thoughts and actions.

In this most supreme hour, the Rêverian nation proclaims its statehood, the worthiness of its august destiny and the poetic necessity under which it was founded.

ALL POWER TO THE IMAGINATION!

signed on behalf of the government of Rêves

On the Street of the Cornered Cat, G. Garfield and I parted. I had no desire to discover if his fantasies were identical to mine, so I waited for him to turn the corner, out of sight, before I telephoned Nadja and arranged for a trip to Murmurs.

THE PLEASURES OF MURMURS IN THE PROVINCE OF MYSTÈRE ARE NOT TO BE DENIED.

THE KASPER HAUSER STARLIGHT EXPRESS

⑥

The train's passengers were a blend of seductive and mysterious strangers. In between embraces, Nadja and I speculated about who they were, their secrets, their desires, and the lives they lived.

"Attention, attention," the loudspeakers intoned, "Mesdames et messieurs, ladies and gentlemen. The Kasper Hauser Express is now boarding on Platform Number Three, making stops at the Tower of Winds, Windows and Mirrors, Rare Flowers, Seven Mysteries, and terminating at Murmurs."

We moved with our fellow unrushed travelers to the platform, and were greeted by the Directeur Général of the Trans-Rêves Line. "Monsieur Victor, and

Mademoiselle Nadja! Mes amis, what a pleasure it is to see you again. It has been far too long." The Directeur Général, gracious as always, inquired about our destination, and said that he would be traveling as far as Candle's Echo in his private Pullman. We turned to board the gleaming deep blue coach with the Trans-Rêves emblem running along its side. Before we boarded, the Chef du Conducteur approached us, dressed in a smart blue uniform.

"Monsieur La Nuages?"

"Oui."

"A telegram, monsieur," he said as he handed me the envelope.

On board, the attendant guided us down a corridor of mirrors, cut glass, polished brass, and dazzling panels of inlaid cherry and walnut. I closed the door to our compartment and opened the telegram. I lit a cigarette and leaned back on one of the burgundy-colored chairs.

"There are two agents on the train," I told Nadja. The train was slowly beginning to move. We passed under the great iron roof of the station, and out into the night. As the train increased its pace, the carriage began to sway gently.

In the dining car a waiter showed us to a table, then he brought us the cocktails that we most desired. He lit the candle on our table and left us with a box of matches. Clearly, we were being looked after. The waiter returned with appetizers: poached love bird eggs in a light crème fraîche sauce, centered by a dollop of black caviar, served with toast points, for Nadja. Two slices of ostrich liver pâté in a shallow pool of flame-red fire lily sauce for me. While the waiter poured us glasses of Chateau de Rêves Vin Blanc, Nadja tasted a laden toast point. A smile came to her lips and her eyes closed in ecstasy. The rich pâté melted in my mouth, blending perfectly with the lightly sweet citric flavor of the sauce. We ate slowly, savoring each morsel. As the entrée was brought in, the wine steward poured a taste of Vintage Château de Rêves Vin Ambrosia Rouge '17, an excellent year. We shared a Chateaubriand, cooked rare and carved at our table, and accompanied by light golden duchess potatoes and baby vegetables. A port wine sauce was ladled over the freshly carved meat. The meal was a feast for the senses.

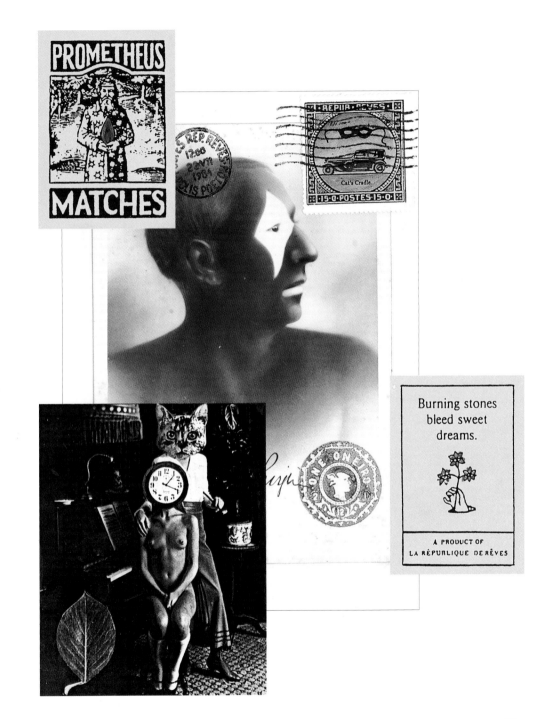

PROMETHEUS MATCHES

Cat's Cradle.
REPUB REVES
15·0·POSTES·15·0

Burning stones
bleed sweet
dreams.

A PRODUCT OF
LA RÉPUBLIQUE DE RÊVES

Dessert was a rich, sumptuous crème brûlée, followed by espresso and a snifter of brandy.

Discreetly we observed the other diners. One man was staring at the bare breasts of a very charming young woman. I didn't like his looks. In a corner sat a very striking raven-haired lady dressed in a handsome deep blue gown embroidered with gold and cut in traditional Rêverian style. Her companion was smartly dressed in tropical whites, American-style. Around his neck he wore a burgundy tie that matched his companion's lips. He glanced toward me. It was Austin Vee! He winked.

When we returned to our coach, I asked the attendant to bring a bottle of Casa Nocito Vin Rouge. When it arrived, I opened the bottle and placed it on the table beneath the window, to let it breathe. We sat back and let the world fade away, as the moon with its generous glow, so bright, moved over us. It bathed the compartment with a magical silver light. We drank in the silence. The rhythmic sway of the moving train, and the muffled clacking of the wheels, peacefully lulled us. The train's whistle echoed through the night, announcing our passage. I poured out two glasses of wine and opened the windows of our deluxe hotel on wheels, allowing us to inhale the perfumes of the night.

⑥

Our mood grew amorous. Outside the window, on the distant horizon, we could see tiny flashes; clusters of fireworks exploding in the star-encrusted sky. "It must be a celebration in Lazy Magnets, probably the Feast of Strong Attractions," Nadja said in a dreamy, sensuous voice. We snuggled together in the seat, our lips slowly met, our thoughts blended.

There was a sharp knocking on the door. "Don't answer it!" she whispered. "Maybe they'll go away." The knocking continued, until I finally answered the door. It was the breast-staring man from the dining car with a small silver revolver in his hand, pointed at me.

"You, G. Garfield Crimmins, will get off the train with me at Seven Mysteries. I am here to rescue you from those," he cast a scornful glance at Nadja, "who have seduced you with imaginings." His tone was crude and arrogant: clearly a member of the League of Common Sense.

"I would offer you some wine, but we only have two glasses," I said courteously.

"Don't worry, I have good no-nonsense whiskey." He pulled a flask from his breast pocket, opening it deftly with one hand. He took a long swig, and placed it on the table. "You know, G. Garfield, 'imagination' is a word people use when they don't know what they are doing." Nadja and I sipped our wine. "These people are our enemies—a cancer of absurd, irrelevant nonconformists who incite our world to question its truths and values. This polluted country is sheltering a conspiracy: a plot to allow invasions of the unconscious, dreams, myths, and illusions! You don't belong here!" Our visitor took another swig from his flask, and sat back. His eyes shifted to Nadja; she had let her wrap fall from her shoulders. Her bare breasts were luminous in the moonlight.

"What you said, it sounds like you really believe it. I like people who believe what they say," she said in a soft voice. A warm breeze from the window made her earrings tinkle. "We have a few hours before we arrive at Seven Mysteries. How about a drink in the club car, the three of us?" she asked sweetly.

"How about it? I feel like a whiskey myself," I said, trying to use an American accent.

⑥

Inside the club car, we were engulfed by an atmosphere of casual celebration. Fumes of rich tobacco rose into the air. Fresh breezes came through the open windows. The carriage was filled with music and the hum of conversation. We sat down at a table and ordered our drinks. At a table not far from ours, there came a high, unrestrained cascade of laughter. Bruder Busch and his wife, Solange, were having an animated conversation with the Directeur of the Trans-Rêves Line and his wife, Mercedes Corporal.

Bruder was, as usual, stylishly dressed in an emerald-green silk suit and vest. The gold chain of his pocket watch ran across his stomach. His smartly waxed mustache twitched as he talked. He gestured with his ever-present walking stick. He had a vast collection of walking sticks, because he habitually misplaced them. Solange was beautiful as always. Her raven hair was cut in a short tight bob that accented her delicately sculpted features. Her shoulders were bare and she wore a necklace of multiple strands of pearls that almost covered her breasts. Her skin glowed.

"I feel like I'm surrounded by a bunch of nut cases headed to the loony bin,"

our companion said. It was obvious that he had never been in such close quarters with so many Rêverians before. As we drank in silence, he scanned the salon discreetly. His gaze settled on a lone woman who sat at the other end of the car. There was a candle on the table which illuminated her face, and a bottle of eau-de-vie. Her gray eyes were clear and cold. She wore typical Rêverian attire, but anyone could see that she was not an islander. The other agent, I thought.

Nadja rose to leave, but our would-be jailer reached over and grabbed her arm. "Where do you think you're going?"

She looked down at him sternly, as if she were about to reproach a child. "Wherever I choose," she said, pulling her arm back. "And right now, I am going to say hello to some friends. You may come along if you would like." She indicated the table where Bruder and the Directeur were seated.

"No, I don't want to meet any more crazies," he responded. "Just remember that I have a gun, so don't do anything stupid."

"Don't be paranoid. Relax! If you didn't worry so much, you'd be much happier." She waved his threat aside.

I signaled to the waiter and ordered more wine. This time the gunman agreed to try it. As he sipped the wine, he asked why I seemed so reluctant to go with him.

"Is it because of that Nadja woman? She is lovely, G. Garfield. Maybe we could take her back with us. She could be assimilated, after she was debriefed."

I could not imagine Nadja in the outer world for any length of time. She was patient, but she had little or no tolerance for the League. She thought they were pompous, childish, and unable to be happy.

"The Directeur has invited us back to his private car, after the stop at Rare Flowers," Nadja said on her return. "We'll be there for several hours, during the height of the Festa di Primavera. It will be something you won't forget." Our companion began to protest, but weakly, as the wine had begun to do its work. He loosened his tie and stared at a striking young woman who had just sat down two tables away from ours. He couldn't keep his eyes off of her. Dressed in the style of

northern Désir, she wore a transparent green silk dress off one shoulder exposing one breast. Her long auburn hair was fashioned in a single braid and covered with a transparent gold veil. Her green eyes twinkled and a mischievous smile played on her lips.

"Why don't you go over and ask her to join us?" Nadja's question caught him off guard and brought his attention back to us.

"What do you mean?"

"Just go ahead. Don't be shy." Nadja prodded him until he finally got up and went over to her table, and was immediately engaged in conversation. As he talked, he somehow appeared to be transformed.

"How much Vin de Rêves did he have?"

"Obviously, just enough." I smiled. "Your plan has begun to work. He will have gone native by the time we reach Seven Mysteries."

Meanwhile, Austin Vee had strolled into the car, looking every bit the dandy that he sometimes was. More than a few women in the car turned their heads as he passed. We listened innocently as he introduced himself to the cold-eyed woman and asked for a light. She handed him a book of matches and introduced herself as Lois Mealy. We listened as Austin began recounting one of his fabled stories.

"Every time my grandmother would tell a tale, each time it was different. One day she fell from a cloud, the next she was in an underwater house dancing with a fish. 'What is the truth, Grandmother?' I would ask. She would laugh at me and say, 'The truth is what you want it to be. The truth is in the words. . . .I was up in the mountains. . . .'"

More passengers entered for nightcaps, greeting and joking with friends and strangers alike, making it difficult to hear what Austin was saying. Still, we watched. It was easy to see that the cold-eyed woman was only tolerating him. The Directeur stopped by our table.

"We're going to be arriving in Rare Flowers soon. You and Nadja will join us at the celebration, won't you, Victor?"

Two citizens of the province of Magie, on the road to mechanical pianos. They were speaking to each other but the photographer did not think there was a family connection.

"We'd like to, but. . . ." I faltered as I glanced over my shoulder at our gunman.

"Don't worry about him. He's with Yvonne Doe, a very accomplished agent of the Society. And I'm sure Austin will perform his usual magic on the other agent. Relax, you're on holiday."

The sounds of music combining with voices in celebration could be heard through the open windows as we prepared to leave the train. The air of the town was filled with the sweet perfumes emitted from roses, honeysuckle, gardenias, fire lilies, and poet's hearts. We found an outdoor café and ordered drinks. People young and old crowded the sidewalks with laughter and shouts of joy, enveloped in the excitement of the fête. Naked and near-naked bodies, dancing, swirled in motion through the streets and parks. People in various stages of undress trooped by waving the tricolored flag of the Rêverian nation; some wore it as a cape. As it neared midnight, we joined the revelers as the party started to spill out onto the Grand Boulevard.

On a stage lit by torches, a man in a bowler and a black-and-white kilt with a red sash started an impassioned speech:

"Either you live someone else's dream or you can live your own!"

This was received by loud cheering. He continued, "There is a difference between our nation and the rest of the world. Everything that is here is there, but here we see the gold in the sun and the silver in the moon and sing to them. We stop to savor the scent of flowers and the sweetness of the fruit. We are not afraid of the beauty of men and women. All that is Rêves, is in all of us!"

A deafening cheer rose up from the crowd. He doffed his bowler and was followed by an explosion that made the ground shudder, as a radiant jewel shot high into the sky. After a second of delay, during which we all held our breath, there was a giant explosion of yellows, crimson, oranges, blues, and purples forming visions of dragons, a phoenix, and giant flowers. They dissolved into showers of sparks, spraying the scents of jasmine and orange blossoms as they fell. The fire

WHEN TWO FRIENDS UNDERSTAND EACH OTHER TOTALLY, THE
WORDS ARE SOFT AND STRONG LIKE AN ORCHIDS PERFUME.
                                              CITIZEN KUNG TSE

works continued for what seemed like hours. At the end of the last explosion, there was only silence, and then a jubilant cheer and applause.

We made our way slowly through the crowds of people to a circle of blazing torches, and waited for the ceremonial lighting of the bonfire by the Minister of Illumination. As soon as it was ignited, the bonfire blazed with sparks whose colors spanned the rainbow, shooting sulfurous spurts of light. Not far from our group in the light of blaze, I saw the LOCS gunman, nearly naked now, and smiling. His eyes shifted from the fire to the woman from Désir. Finally the two embraced with abandon. I nudged Nadja, who smiled.

Back on board the train a telegram was waiting for me.

NGER SERVICE

RAM

MURMURS

At dawn the train pulled into the station at Seven Mysteries. The scent of ripening grapes permeated the air. The station itself was a large grape arbor. Honey bees buzzed in and out of the vines. We were in the wine-producing region of Rêves. There the Brotherhood of the Knights of the Vine is sworn to defend the vines and the secrets of wine making.

Nadja had woken just as the train was getting underway again. After showering and dressing, we went to the dining car, and took a table by a window. In the center of the table was a vase of flowers and a large bowl of grapes. A distinguished-looking elderly gentleman entered the car.

He introduced himself as Domenick Nicito, Master Wine Maker, and asked to join our table.

"You see, nothing gives itself so entirely as the vine. It can be eaten," he said as he plucked a grape from the bowl. "It can be drunk." He produced a bottle from his basket and set it on the table. "You can sit in its shade, its leaf can be stuffed and eaten, and when it dies, it can even be burned for warmth. This bottle is for you; I can foresee you will be good company."

We had a light breakfast of coffee, grapes, peaches, some cheese and biscuits. We chatted as the train glided through the hills and slopes of Seven Mysteries. In every direction, the vineyards glistened in the morning dew. The day was sparkling, the smell of the countryside heady and intoxicating. The occasional dwellings that the train passed all had gardens in full bloom. The flowers were as tall as trees. Among the blossoms and foliage children climbed and played. Everywhere we saw diligent poets in the fields gathering dreams. Large trumpet blossoms of honeysuckle oozed sweet nectar, which dripped and glistened in the clear light. Massive pink and white lady slippers gave off a rich vanilla scent. The air was a tapestry of sweet rich aromas and sights.

As we neared our destination everyone on board went to the windows to look out. No one wanted to miss the entrance to Murmurs. The old Rêverian town was wrapped in a gauze of fog, the gables and turrets of its Victorian architecture poking out like candles in the mist. As the train slowly entered the station, we were welcomed by a band playing a Hungarian rhapsody. We collected our luggage, and said good-bye to our friends. The Directeur and his wife were going on to Bewitching Birds before heading back to Echoes and Sighs. The sun had burned off the fog as we walked up the steps of the turreted Hôtel de Paris. Our room had a balcony which overlooked the Bay of Sunflowers. The bed was situated in the center, between the three windows of the turret bay. A full-length mirror stood off to the side. The room was designed for sleeping, dreaming, and lovemaking. Our bags were placed neatly by the bed. I sat on the bed and began to disrobe. Nadja removed her dress. I watched, transfixed by her beauty, as

she stood in front of the mirror. She smiled and walked over to me, placing her hands on my shoulders as she bent down to kiss me. Her nipples brushed my face as she rose and said, "Come on, Victor, I'm starving."

"Me too," I smiled. I watched as she stepped into a pale yellow muslin skirt, which hung low on her hips.

Outside, the sun was warm and a light breeze drifted in from the ocean. The streets were not crowded, but neither were they empty. We walked down the sun-dappled sidewalks, shaded by palm and date trees. The architecture was high Victorian in pastel blues, reds, and yellows. The residents, dressed in transparent garments, were relaxed and unhurried. We walked a few blocks, and then turned

MURMURS, RELAXING ON THE
BEACH OF SOFT VOICES, AND
SURFING ON THE BAY OF
SUNFLOWERS.

up a side street and found an open-air market. Nadja picked a red, plump straw-berry from a cart and put it to my lips.

"Taste it. Tell me if it's sweet."

As I bit into the fruit, its sweetness exploded in my mouth. Along with the strawberries, we bought grapes and oranges. As we moved through the market, its heady, dizzying smells of fresh-baked breads, fresh fruit, exotic spices and flowers washed over us. Nadja argued good-naturedly with the cheese merchant in Italian. Then she moved on to a bread cart.

"Deux baguettes, s'il vous plaît." Nadja loved to shop in an open-air market; her stamina seemed to have no bounds. Soon her arms were full of bags, and she was exhilarated.

"Let's get some wine, maybe some champagne. We'll take a carriage back to the hotel."

Entering our suite, we found it brilliantly illuminated with shafts of the afternoon sun. I poured myself a brandy, lit a cigarette, and sank into one of the captain's chairs. As I exhaled I watched the smoke dissolve into the sunlight. I could hear Nadja showering. After finishing my cigarette, I went out onto the balcony and sipped my brandy. Beneath me was a small park, where a woman and two young girls ambled lazily through an area of shady trees, and then into a sun-drenched clearing. In the distance, a raven cawed. The girls began to do somersaults and cartwheels. I applauded their acrobatics; they laughed and bowed and then continued their tumblings. I could feel the sea and smell the salt air. Elsewhere in the park an orchestra was playing Vivaldi's <u>The Four Seasons</u>. The music drew me in, and I felt time slipping away. The smell of sandalwood drew me out of my reverie. There stood Nadja smiling, looking radiant in a flowing white shift that opened at the side.

I too showered, groaning with pleasure as the hot water ran down my body, over every tired muscle. Out of the shower and dry, I put on a light blue gauze tunic. In the living area, Nadja was pouring wine as I came out of the bedroom. We sat down to a meal of fruit, cheese, and bread, then moved out to the balcony to have our wine. It was cooler now; the sun was lower in the reddened sky. A soft breeze made Nadja's hair a fluffy cloud. The city glowed in pastel pinks, blues, and greens.

Nadja slipped her arm around my waist and gently rested her head on my shoulder. "Let's go inside. I feel like going to bed. Get the champagne," she whispered. I retrieved the bucket and some glasses, and found her standing by the open bay window. The setting sunlight shone through her almost transparent shift, setting off the darkness of her nipples and pubis against the white, gauzy silk. She was combing out her hair with her fingertips. Her eyes sparkled as she flashed me a mischievously coy smile. The soft strains of Debussy's <u>Prelude to "The Afternoon of a Faun"</u> drifted in the background. I watched her as she crossed the room with an easy, sensual grace, the soft curves of her body tantalizingly revealed by the semi-opaqueness of her gown.

NOTSOBAD AND PRETTYNICE GATHER THE NIGHT'S DREAMS AS REASON AND LOGIC WATCH.
—THE BOOK OF TORMANDS, VOL. V, LEAF #25.

"Champagne, mademoiselle?," I asked, displaying the ice bucket.

"Oui, merci beaucoup." She took my hand and gave it a squeeze. "The bed looks inviting and comfortable, monsieur." She sat on the bed and pulled me down next to her.

The champagne was opened, poured out, and we drank it as we lay together and listened to the music. Then Nadja reached over and took the glass out of my hand; along with hers, she placed it on the table by the bed. She looked into my eyes. She let her shift fall from her shoulders, and deftly undid my tunic. She drew herself to me, I could feel the warmth of her body against mine. We kissed with an ever-increasing intensity, and caressed each other's bodies. Our flesh melted together, and we slowly made love, as if in a dream. As we returned to consciousness, Nadja said softy, "I missed you so much, Victor."

"Nadja, mon amour, I love you." A soft breeze bathed our bodies as we drifted off into a peaceful slumber.

When we awoke, moonlight flooded the bedroom. Nadja put her arms around me, and we kissed. Her hair was matted and disheveled, her face had a reddish glow. "Nadja, you're beautiful."

"I'm hungry," she said with a dreamy smile. I could not stop myself from laughing.

⑥

It was a fine night, a wonderful night. The moon lit the city in a pale blue light. We walked hand in hand down the cobblestone streets of Murmurs. Young and old people sat on benches in the park, watching the nightlife of the city. They were whispering, kissing, murmuring. In alcoves, in alleyways, and among the trees in the park, there were couples in embrace. Strangers came up to bid us a cheery good evening, in a medley of languages. "The Fête of Whispers and Sighs, the lovers' festival, Victor," Nadja whispered to me as we walked several more blocks,

'till we came to the entrance of the Café L'indigo. At the door we were greeted by Jean, who embraced us and called out to Johanna, who was at the bar. "Come, Johanna, see what the winds of chance have blown in." Johanna, the owner and operator of the café, came over and greeted us as warmly as Jean had. He showed us to an empty table, ordered us a bottle of Vin de Rêves, and raised a toast: "May the sun and moon shine upon your faces. May the winds of chance be always at your backs. May all clocks fall under the spell of the waterfall. To you, Victor and Nadja, to your health and to your dreams."

Then Jean grew serious as he told us about a strange individual who had

been in the café in the afternoon. "He was immaculately dressed, but there was something wrong and odd about him. He was extremely unfriendly, as cold as a stone. I can truly say that I disliked him on sight. But enough," he proclaimed, "you are hungry and it is the night of the Lovers' Festival." He took our order and disappeared.

We ate slowly, savoring each bit of culinary magic. Our conversation was going this way and that, touching on poetry, art, and embracing life. We spoke of a poet we had once seen pulling bits and pieces of light from his pockets. We lin-

gered over cognac, and coffee. The café was almost full, musical with quiet laughter and the hum of conversation. Nicole, Dr. Prometheus' assistant, came into the café on the arm of a beautiful man, whom she introduced as Apesos, a magician and poet.

"What a night it is!" he exclaimed happily. "The sky is smiling like a fool in love, the umbrella is speaking to the salt shaker, the lamp and the valise are embracing, and the phone is making love to the shoe."

Nicole squeezed her companion's hand, and the two of them smiled warmly at each other. A waiter took them to their table, and we watched them as Apesos took a flower from a vase, slowly removed its petals, reassembled it, and presented it to Nicole.

To our surprise, in came Dr. Prometheus. He found our table, leaned over, and whispered, "Maybe it's time I retired. I could be an architect again; my sister always said it was better to be a practical dreamer and survive." His voice was mellow and clear like a glass tear; he looked as if he had lost something.

Then Jean came over and whispered to me. "The strange man I was telling you about is sitting at the bar." I looked over and recognized him immediately. In one smooth gesture he drew a revolver from his jacket pocket and took aim at me.

At that moment, the patrons sitting around the bar immediately and simultaneously broke into a song of one pure, rich note. The rest of the diners in the restaurant joined in. The song comes from the depths of the collective Rêverian soul. To native Rêverian ears, it is unadulterated pleasure, but to non-Rêverians it is devastating in its effect. It is the song of defense. It started out soft and low, and then slowly built in pitch and volume, filling the restaurant with a vibration that caused the glasses to shake and tremble. The pistol in the man's hand began to quiver, and then his arm started to twitch, and soon his entire body was convulsing in spasms. His expression changed from determined confidence to fear. Finally, the gun fell from his hand as he covered his ears to block the sound, and he screamed; not in fear, but in failure. Then he collapsed on the floor, exhausted. The restaurant grew still. We went over to the bar immediately. The hat that the agent had been wearing had fallen off, and it was apparent that the "man" had not been a man at all, but none other than Lois Mealy, the cold-eyed woman from the train in disguise. She glared at me defiantly, and snarled, "You're a fool. The whole lot of you are insane." Officers from Sûreté arrived almost immediately, and took her into custody.

"In the future, we must never be overconfident in our dealing with these people," Dr. Prometheus said in a serious voice. "Even when unintelligent they can be very clever."

"Doctor, we mustn't let you get depressed," Jean said, and to cheer him, suggested a celebration in the opulent, spacious, intimate rooms of the H.H. Club on the second floor of the café.

Upstairs the lighting was subdued, and there were mirrors everywhere: on the walls and the ceiling. Fish with long feathered tails swam through the air, and shooting stars played across the ceiling. Couples sprawled on rich crimson sofas in alcoves shaped like letters of the Greek alphabet, talking in hushed voices, quietly laughing and kissing. Curtains were sometimes drawn across the openings for privacy. Our party made themselves comfortable on couches surrounding the dance floor and drank champagne. The night progressed into relaxed frivolity, and we danced, euphoric.

It was well past midnight by the time we returned to the hotel. Before retiring, Nadja and I sat in the hotel garden. The moon above was full in a black sky of faint stars and one bright planet. The dew was heavy and pearled. It was still very warm, with the only noise coming from the music of the murmuring water in the pond, the

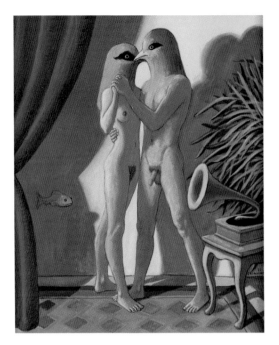

Like love, each day is forever being reborn,
with chance and imagination as the
main ingredients.
—Anrig the Great

chirping of the night birds, and the occasional rustling of the leaves as a light breeze moved through the trees. Leaning against me, Nadja said dreamingly, "This is only the beginning, Victor. Who knows what tomorrow will bring?"

THE EPILOGUE

It is two o'clock in the morning, the second of May, 1996. My apartment is absolutely still; the only noise is that of the occasional hum of the refrigerator and the ticking of the clock on the wall. I just finished reading what I have set down. Again I looked at the envelope postmarked "la République de Rêves." I remember receiving it when I had been in my Philadelphia apartment for just a few months. It had made little impression on me at the time. My life had become totally absorbed in my teaching and the academic world I had entered. I worked and lived in an ivory tower, where such things as happened in Rêves could only happen in dreams.

Soon, however, I started to feel worn down by the madness of academic politics, inflated egos, and countless meetings where I never ceased to be amazed at the number of ways my colleagues found to pontificate about nothing of substance over and over again, for hours and hours on end. Increasingly, good sense was replaced by commonsense solutions and explanations of things. Every day I was asked by someone, "What happened to your common sense?" Then I remembered who I was dealing with, why my life was seeming oppressive—the intrigues of the LOCS.

While going through the flotsam and jetsam of my papers, I happened across Victor La Nuage's letter to me. This time I read it slowly and carefully. I leaned back in my chair and lit a cigarette, letting my thoughts drift. I remembered storing all of my Rêverian memorabilia, a tourist guide, maps, my journal, and Rêverian passport. Toward the end of his letter, Victor had asked me when I would be returning to the island.

That was the night that I had the first of many dreams which would bring me back to la République de Rêves. With each successive night, my dreams became more vivid. Soon the dreams spilled over into my waking state. At times, it seemed I was dreaming when I was awake, and awake when I was dreaming. Finally, I felt compelled to assemble this record of my recollections. I ask myself the question: Do we lead parallel lives? One when we are awake and one when we are dreaming? In my dreams, I am Victor La Nuage, and when I am awake and open the passport I find Victor's name beneath my much younger likeness. I remember being totally alive then, as in no other time in my memory. In my hand is a one-oneiro gold coin. It is heavier than most coinage. As I caress it, and turn it in my fingers, an image appears in my mind of skipping its double out onto the sparkling waters of Lake Eros, and watching it glitter in the sun before it disappeared into the water. I close my eyes and smile. I know that I will return. Out through the window, even in the darkness of the night, the blossoms of the dogwood tree glow, even as they do on the island, and I can smell the scent of wisteria and roses.

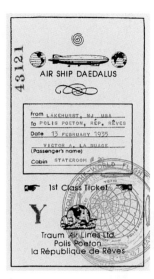

AIR SHIP DAEDALUS

43121

From LAKEHURST, NJ, USA
To POLIS POETON, RÉP. RÊVES
Date 13 FEBRUARY 1935
       VICTOR A. LA NUAGE
(Passenger's name)
Cabin STATEROOM # 29

1st Class Ticket

Y

Traum Air Lines Ltd.
Polis Poeton
la République de Rêves

I am sending this to remind you
That my address remains the same.